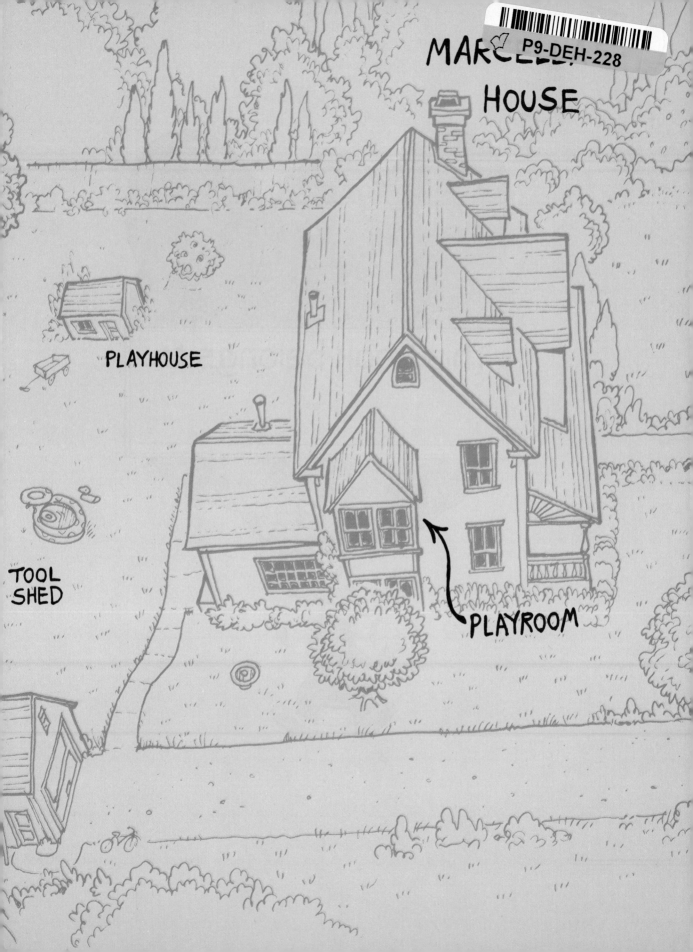

This book belongs to:

_____

*Raggedy Ann & Andy's*

# THE BOX OF TRICKS

A LYNX BOOK

This book is published by Lynx Books, a division of Lynx Communications, Inc., 41 Madison Avenue, New York, New York 10010. The name "Lynx" together with the logotype consisting of a stylized head of a lynx is a trademark of Lynx Communications, Inc.

Raggedy Ann and Andy's Grow-and-Learn Library, the names and depictions of Raggedy Ann, Raggedy Andy and all related characters are trademarks of Macmillan, Inc.

Marcella walked into her playroom carrying a big shopping bag.

"What a great birthday party I've had!" she told her dolls. "Just wait until you see all the wonderful presents I got!"

First she showed Babette the French Doll a lovely new doll dress that was just Babette's size. "This present is really for both of us," Marcella said.

Marcella tried the dress on Babette. Babette was so excited that she wished she could see herself in the mirror.

Then Marcella took a pretty bottle out of the shopping bag. She opened it and held it up to Raggedy Ann's nose.

"Yuck!" thought Raggedy Andy. "Perfume! I hope she doesn't come near me with that!"

Next Marcella took a jigsaw puzzle out of the bag. "Great!" thought Percy the Policeman Doll, who enjoyed putting a puzzle together almost as much as he enjoyed solving a mystery.

Then Marcella took out a top and spun it on the playroom floor.

As Percy watched the top spin round and round, he got so dizzy he almost fell over.

Then Marcella took out a little basketball hoop and a soft rubber ball. Sunny Bunny watched happily as Marcella attached the hoop to the side of the shelf. He could hardly wait to try a game of basketball.

"I got a new storybook, too," said Marcella, holding it up for them to see.

"This is the best present of all," thought The Camel with the Wrinkled Knees, who would rather listen to a bedtime story than do almost anything else.

Raggedy Ann was pleased, too, since she loved to read Marcella's books to the other dolls.

"And this is a box of tricks," she said, placing the box on the toy shelf.

That night, when Marcella and her family were asleep, the dolls popped out of their beds and ran to the shelf to look at the new toys—except for Babette, who headed straight for the mirror.

Bubbles and Sunny Bunny played with the top while
Raggedy Ann and The Camel looked through the new
book.

Greta the Dutch Doll and Percy took down the new puzzle and began putting the pieces together.

Raggedy Andy took the box of tricks over to the window seat. He reached into the box and, one by one, took out the things inside. His button eyes almost popped out of his head when he thought about how much fun he'd have playing little tricks on everyone!

Bubbles and Sunny Bunny had grown tired of playing with the top, so Bubbles put it back on the shelf.

"How about playing a game of basketball?" Sunny Bunny called to Raggedy Andy.

"Maybe later," said Raggedy Andy absentmindedly. "I'm busy right now."

"Okay," thought Sunny Bunny, who decided to ask Greta and Tim to join him instead.

Raggedy Andy was almost ready to begin the fun.

He slipped out to the bathroom sink and was back in a minute. Then he looked around the room for Babette.

"Hey, Babette," he called to her. "You sure look pretty in your new dress! How would you like me to take your picture?"

"My picture?" said Babette in surprise. "Why, yes. That would be perfect," she said with a toss of her curls.

"Are you ready?" asked Raggedy Andy as Babette fluffed up her bonnet and smoothed out her dress. "Say cheese," he said sweetly.

He held up the camera, pressed the button, and out shot a stream of water—all over Babette.

"Got you!" shouted Raggedy Andy, laughing so hard that he almost lost his balance.

"My new dress is all wet!" cried Babette. "How could you do that?"

"It will dry fine," Raggedy Andy said, chuckling to himself.

Raggedy Ann gave her brother a puzzled look. Then she went over to Babette to help her dry off.

By this time most of the other dolls were laughing. Raggedy Dog was howling loudest of all.

Raggedy Andy searched through the box for just the right trick to try next. When he found what he was looking for, he called to Raggedy Dog.

"Want a bone?" he asked, tossing one on the floor.

"Sure!" shouted Raggedy Dog, giving a happy little bark. Taking a big leap, Raggedy Dog grabbed for the bone, but he was too late. The bone was attached to a string. Just as Raggedy Dog was about to pounce, Raggedy Andy yanked it away.

"Nice try," laughed Raggedy Andy as Raggedy Dog skidded across the floor.

Raggedy Dog didn't think Raggedy Andy was very funny this time!

Raggedy Andy went back to his box full of tricks and took out some jumping beans. Then he quietly sneaked over to Raggedy Cat. He took a ball of yarn and stuck a fistful of jumping beans inside it.

"Wake up, Raggedy Cat. I have a surprise for you," he said, setting the ball of yarn down in front of her nose.

Raggedy Cat crouched down. Her nose twitched in excitement as she got ready to play her favorite game. But as soon as she struck, the ball of yarn jumped out of her way.

Arching her back, she let out a frightened "meow!" and scampered under the toy box to hide.

"Ha! Ha! Ha!" laughed Raggedy Andy, holding his sides.

"How did you do that?" asked Percy.

"Jumping beans," said Raggedy Andy proudly. "Neat trick, right?"

"Just don't go trying any of that stuff on me," Percy warned.

"Okay," said Raggedy Andy. "It's a deal. Let's shake on it."

Percy reached for Raggedy Andy's hand. He grabbed it and . . .

*Bzzzzzz!*

"What's that?" Percy cried, jumping back in alarm.

"I zapped you," laughed Raggedy Andy, "with my hand buzzer!"

"I don't like your tricks," said Percy.

"Oh, come on. They're pretty funny," said Raggedy Andy, not paying a bit of attention.

"They are not!" said Babette.

"Not funny at all," said Raggedy Cat.

"I think you should stop teasing everybody," Raggedy Ann told him. "Don't you see that you're the only one who's having any fun?"

"I can't believe it," replied Raggedy Andy. "Where is your sense of humor?" He turned and strolled away from his friends.

Sunny Bunny, Greta, and Tim the Toy Soldier were still shooting baskets.

Raggedy Andy climbed on the shelf above the basketball hoop. He sat there for a while, cheering his friends on as they played. But then, without warning, he pulled out a little box.

Just as Sunny Bunny was about to throw the ball,
Raggedy Andy sprinkled some powder into the air.
*"Achoo!"* sneezed Sunny Bunny.
He missed his shot.

Tim didn't see what happened.

"My turn," he called out. But just as he was ready to shoot the ball into the basket, Raggedy Andy sprinkled a little powder near him, too.

"*Achoo!*" sneezed Tim. "*Achoo! Achoo! Achoo!*"

By now Greta had caught on.

"Put that sneezing powder away!" she said angrily. "You're ruining the game!"

"Yeah," sniffed Tim between sneezes. "It's not funny at all!"

Raggedy Andy went back to the window seat.
"I don't know what's wrong with everybody," he
thought to himself. "Why are they acting so grouchy? After
all, I didn't hurt anybody. I only wanted to have a little fun.
What's their problem anyway?"

Raggedy Andy looked into his box of tricks again. There was one trick he hadn't tried yet.

He lifted it out of the box and studied it. It was a can with a picture of worms on the lid.

"This is great!" thought Raggedy Andy, starting to feel better already. "I'll take one of these fake worms and put it in Raggedy Ann's pocket. I can't wait to see her face when she finds it!"

Raggedy Ann was reading a story to the other dolls, who were gathered around her. After each page, she would hold up the book so that everyone could see the pictures.

"This is my chance," thought Raggedy Andy. "The next time Raggedy Ann holds up the book, I'll sneak over and slip one of these into her apron pocket."

He slowly and quietly began to open the can. All of a sudden, the lid flew off—and out shot three long, wiggly worms.

"*Pop! Pop! Pop!*" they sprang.

Raggedy Andy was so startled that he fell off the window seat with a loud cry!

The fake worms lay in a heap beside him.

"What happened?" he shouted.

But no one could hear him. They were laughing much too loud!

"It's not very funny!" cried Raggedy Andy, who was feeling kind of foolish.

"You're right," said Raggedy Ann gently. "Now you know how everyone else has been feeling."

"But it's not fun when the joke is on *me*," said Raggedy Andy sheepishly.

"That's what I mean," said Raggedy Ann.

"I'm really sorry," Raggedy Andy told the other dolls.

"We forgive you, Raggedy Andy," said Percy, "but on one condition . . ."

"I know. I know," interrupted Raggedy Andy. "I promise—no more practical jokes!"

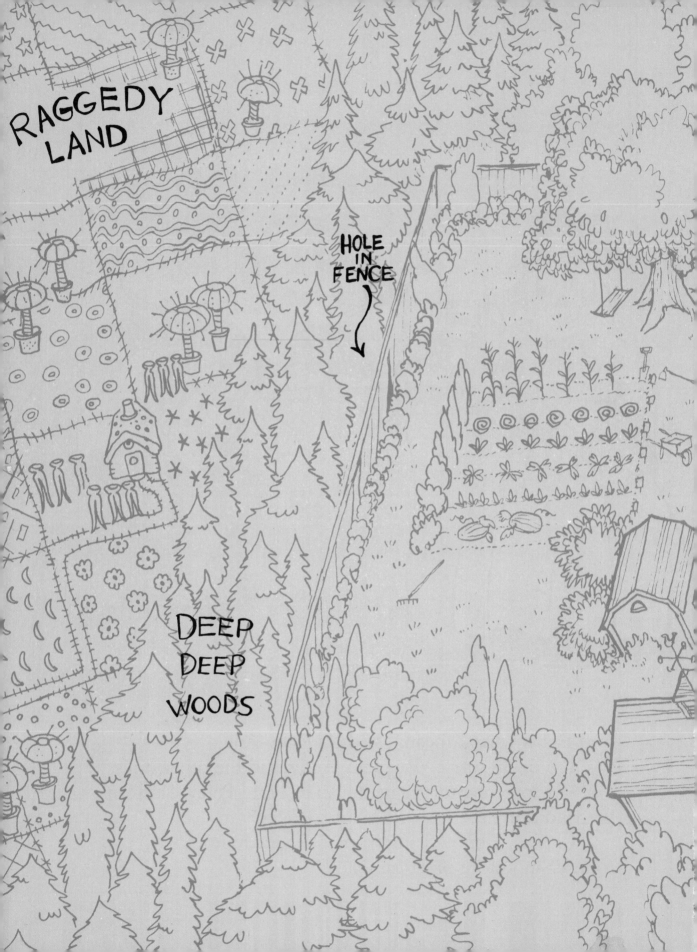